For my mama,
who taught me to love growing

ABOUT THIS BOOK

The illustrations for this book were done in pencil, colored pencil, watercolor pencil, and watercolor ink on Strathmore wet illustration board. This book was edited by Nikki Garcia and designed by Patrick Collins with art direction from Saho Fujii. The production was supervised by Patricia Alvarado, and the production editor was Annie McDonnell. The text was set in Aged Book, and the display type is hand-lettered.

Hachette Book Group • 1290 Avenue of the Americas, New York, NY 10104 • Visit us at LBYR.com • First Edition: April 2022 • Little, Brown and Company is a division of Hachette Book Group, Inc. • The Little, Brown name and logo are trademarks of Hachette Book Group, Inc. • The publisher is not responsible for websites (or their content) that are not owned by the publisher. • Library of Congress Cataloging-in-Publication Data • Names: Pray, Faith, author, illustrator. • Title: Perfectly imperfect Mira / by Faith Pray. • Description: First edition. | New York : Little, Brown and Company, 2022. | Audience: Ages 4-8. | Summary: Mira wants to be good at something, but she is held back by her desire to be perfect. • Identifiers: LCCN 2021011137 | ISBN 9780316541169 (hardcover) • Subjects: CYAC: Perfectionism (Personality trait)–Fiction. | Growth–Fiction. • Classification: LCC PZ7.1.P6993 Pe 2022 | DDC [E]–dc23 • LC record available at https://lccn.loc.gov/2021011137 • ISBN 978-0-316-54116-9 • PRINTED IN CHINA • APS • 10 9 8 7 6 5 4 3 2 1

perfectly imperfect MIRA

FAITH PRAY

L B

LITTLE, BROWN AND COMPANY
New York   Boston

Mira wanted to be good at something, but everyone else was already better. Everyone else was already a natural.

Every time Mira started a new thing, she gave up.

Mira never got to the second of anything.

Not the second day.

Not the second lesson.

Not the second try.

Mira wanted every try
to be perfect.
But it wasn't.

What if she fell?
What if people laughed?
What if she did it the wrong way?

So, while other kids tumbled and spun and sprang, Mira stayed still.

They were mountains.
Mira was a stone.

They were rivers.
Mira was a trickle.

They were trees.
Mira was a seed.

Let them be perfect, Mira thought.
I will be a stone.
I will be a trickle.
I will be a seed.

Or maybe just a shadow.

But staying a shadow meant...
No twirls.
No splashes.
No laughs.
Mira's feet longed to stretch.
Even just a wiggle.

Mira wondered.
What would it be like to pretend
to be good at something...
just for a minute?

She checked to make sure
no one was watching...

Wobbled...
and did it all wrong.
But it felt better than
being a shadow.

What would it be like to do
that a second time?

That one was a humongous flop.
Good thing no one was watching.

Oh.

Well. It wasn't so terrible.
Doing something.

What if she tried again?

This time, Mira unfurled, untucked, and uncurled.

Not quite...
But that one felt almost like a laugh.

Mira tried again.

She bounced.

She stumbled.

She spun and sprang.

It wasn't perfect.
But Mira did it.

And this feeling?

It was almost like becoming a mountain
or a river or a tree.
And Mira loved it.

Mira wanted to be good at something.
And she was.

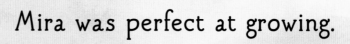

Mira was perfect at growing.

WITHDRAWN